UNTAPPED MELODY

EMMA BRAY

CHAPTER 1

Melody

I PRESS my thighs together and bite my lip. It does nothing to ease the ache in my bladder. I still have to pee just as badly. I don't know why we think crossing our legs will keep us from peeing all over ourselves because it certainly won't. Trust me. I know.

"What's wrong with you, Melody?" Lila asks.

I glare at her. "I told you thirty minutes ago. I've got to freaking pee. You wouldn't pull over the car. You assured me they had restrooms here, but I have yet to see any."

Lila shrugs, unsympathetic to my plight. "You shouldn't have drunk all that sweet tea at dinner."

I ignore her and hop from one foot to the other—as if that will help. I already know it doesn't. It makes matters worse because it jostles my tender bladder.

The other girls are twittering and giggling amongst themselves as they swoon over all the band members we're seeing tonight. Fallen Angels is the hottest band on the music scene right now, but I couldn't tell you one of their songs. I'm not a fan of modern rock music.

The oldies, yeah, I'm all into that. I know I'm weird, but I've never cared for my generation's music. I've always loved hits from the '80s, classical music, and opera. Throw in musicals and, oh boy. It's a varied and eclectic mix, and I'm a total weirdo, as my roommate so kindly pointed out to me before she insisted I come with her and her friends to this rock concert.

There are five of us here, yet somehow, I feel like a third wheel. I don't fit in. This isn't my thing. I should have stayed back at the dorm.

This type of music is not my jam, and I'm the youngest one in the group. I'm nineteen, whereas the other girls are twenty-one, so while they're old enough to buy alcohol, I'm not. They insisted they'd sneak me some on the side, but I'm too much of a coward to break the law.

I'm mid-bounce when one of the security guards manning the arena finally opens the red cord and starts letting fans pour in.

"Come on!" Lila grabs my hand. "We need to hurry and hit the floor to get a good place in front of the stage."

"Lila, I have got to pee, or I'm going to piss all over myself," I hiss at my roommate. Lila frowns at me. I shake my head and pull my hand away from her. "You guys go on. I'll meet up with you later."

They share a skeptical glance before they shrug and head toward the floor.

Lila turns back to me and assures me, "I'll save you a spot, okay? Just be as fast as you can."

"Got it." I wave at her, not caring if I even sit with them at this point. The only thing on my mind is relieving my bladder. If I can't find them afterward, I'm okay with calling a rideshare to take me back to the dorm room.

"Bathroom?" I yell at one of the security dudes. I don't know if he can hear me over the crowd, but he points to the left.

I make my way through the throng of people to where he pointed, scanning for any sign of a bath-room. This place is so packed we're like sardines in a can, and it's all I can do to make my way to a hallway where the crowd thins out.

I breathe a sigh of relief when there are no longer any bodies pressed right up against me. Several doors line the left and right sides of the hallway, and I don't have a clue which one is the bathroom. Maybe they're all bathrooms. I'm seriously fixing to piss all over myself, so I turn the doorknob to one with a funny-looking symbol, hoping it means "women's bathroom."

I stumble into the space and barely glance at it, although my quick observation tells me it's some sort of fancy bathroom. There's a couch and a mirror set up and what looks like a clothing rack in the corner. I pay little attention, heading straight for the back, where another door is wide open. Holy mother of God, I see a flash of porcelain in there.

I flick on the light. "Thank you, Jesus!" I scream in jubilation.

I close the door and hurry over to plant my ass on the porcelain throne and take care of business. I sigh dramatically as I relieve myself. God, I don't think I've ever had to pee so bad in my entire life.

When I'm done, I pull my pants up and move to the sink to wash my hands. I notice the hand soap isn't the cheap, icky kind you usually find in a public bathroom. I bring it to my nose and sniff. It smells like an expensive men's cologne. Sandalwood and citrus.

I shrug and wash my hands. Maybe this venue is more than meets the eye, and they want to treat their patrons to a bit of luxury.

Or maybe I came into the men's bathroom instead of the women's.

Oh, well. There's no one else here, so I'll be in and out in a jiff.

I open the door to the bathroom and jump back with a gasp. A pair of startling green eyes stare at me from the other side of the door. I'm so startled, my heart thunders in my ribcage.

I tilt my head back because the male figure in front of me is impossibly tall with broad shoulders and stylishly shaggy black hair hanging down either side of his face. He's wearing distressed jeans and a white T-shirt underneath a leather jacket.

I swallow. Hard. He's the hottest guy I've ever seen, and it's just my luck to run into him in the men's bathroom.

"S-Sorry!" I stammer. "I thought this was the women's bathroom but it must be the men's and I didn't mean to get in your way so if you'll excuse me I'll get out of here and give you some privacy." I suck in a breath and my cheeks flame. I always word vomit when I'm embarrassed. Either that or freeze up.

I try to sidestep the huge wall of hotness, but he moves with me, stepping to the side to block me from leaving. I look up at him with wide eyes, feeling like a cornered rabbit.

The man's green eyes stay unwaveringly focused on me, and his mouth twitches. "What's your name, beautiful?"

Oh, my god. His voice is like liquid velvet. It's smooth and beautiful and sends a tingle of awareness running up my spine.

I flush as I gaze up at him, completely stupefied. I don't know if a member of the opposite sex has ever called me beautiful—at least not to my face—and this walking mass of testosterone has me all tied up in knots.

"Melody," I say softly.

"Melody," he repeats.

My name sounds like music on his lips. Speaking of lips, his are full and lush and sinful-looking. His green orbs trail down over my face and stop on my mouth, and my face grows even hotter.

"Your name?" I prompt. Not only am I talking out of nervousness, but I truly am dying to know the name of this god.

A flicker of surprise lights his eyes before he answers. "Xavier." He studies my face intently as he tells me his name.

Somehow, I manage to hold his gaze, despite my nervousness. "Are you here for the concert too, Xavier?" I ask lamely.

He stares at me for a beat, his eyes flaring with something I can't identify when I say his name, but then his lips twitch, and his eyes sparkle with amusement. I flush harder when I realize he's probably laughing at me for being so stupid. Of course, he's here for the concert. That's why everyone is here.

"Yeah," he answers simply as he continues to stare at me.

I become fidgety under his gaze. I don't know what to say. This man is too gorgeous, and I don't know how to act. I'm just stupid, silly little me.

I pull at the hem of the denim miniskirt Lila loaned me but immediately regret it when it draws the hot guy's gaze. "Yeah. Okay, nice to meet you, Xavier. I should probably get back to my friends. They're supposed to save me a seat in the front."

"Oh?" He raises an eyebrow. "Are you a big fan of the band?"

I can't stop the laugh that tumbles out of me. "Hardly. I've never even heard them, and new age rock isn't my style."

He grins slowly. "Yeah?"

I flush again as I realize I've probably said too much. "My friends love Fallen Angels and begged me to come with them, so…" I trail off and shrug as if that explains everything.

He smiles, and sweet baby Jesus. It's a full-throttle heartbreaker smile. His teeth are white and even, and the stubble on his jawline only lends to his dark allure. "Well, maybe I'll see you after the concert, and you can let me know what you think of the band."

"Okay, yeah, sure," I tell him, my gaze captured by his.

His mouth twitches again. "Well, you better get out there, beautiful, if you want to make sure you get a good view of the lead singer."

I let out a laugh and scoff, "I'm no groupie."

He levels me with an assessing look. "No, I don't think you are."

With that strange comment, he finally steps aside, though he doesn't leave much room, and my body grazes his as I slip past him. I look up to find his emerald eyes staring at me unwaveringly. I can't decipher the look in them, but it causes my breath to hitch and my palms to sweat.

I quickly look away and hurry to the door. With one final glance over my shoulder, I see his green gaze still trained on me.

Forget the lead singer. Xavier from the bathroom has him beat times a million.

CHAPTER 2

Xavier

I SCAN the crowd from backstage, looking for the pretty little brunette with the soft chocolate-brown eyes.

Melody.

My Melody.

Christ, even her name is perfect, a prediction of how in tune we're going to be.

My lips quirk when I remember how she busted into my dressing room and made a beeline for the bathroom. So intent was she in her search for the toilet that she didn't even see me in the corner of the room. I'd normally be upset at the breach in security—no one should have been able to bust their way into the lead singer's dressing room—but it's the last thing on my mind. Instead, I'm grateful she was thrown into my universe.

I let out a full-fledged laugh when I remember her cry of relief. The chick must have had to pee bad. Hey, no judgment here. We all know what that's like.

I sober when I recall the full assault of those brown eyes looking into mine. She was so innocent. So perfect.

And best of all, she had no clue who I was.

Call me a spoiled rock star, but I'm sick and tired of groupies throwing themselves at me, wanting to sleep with me because of my talent or fame. It's tiring. I want someone to want me for *me*. Not my name or who they think I am. Not the rock star persona, but *me*. Xavier Kane, the man.

I frown when I realize I didn't get Melody's last name. Oh, well. I'll rectify that soon enough because I intend to learn everything there is to know about Melody.

She's such a cute little thing. Her head barely reaches my chest. She's petite yet has delectable curves in all the right places. She's no blonde bombshell. Her beauty is more refined, more classic, and despite the new age shit I sing, I've always been a lover of the classics.

My manager cautioned me against sharing that information in my interviews so I don't confuse my demographic. Keep to the stereotypical rock star persona. Maintain the bad boy image of partying all night long and only caring about rock music. God forbid a rock star enjoys a good opera from time to time.

Something about Melody calls to mind a sweet symphony. What kind of music does she like? She made it clear she's not into popular music, and she's never heard one of my band's songs. I don't know what it says about me, but I find that a huge turn-on. Shouldn't I want a woman who appreciates my art? Not one who's only here because her friends dragged her here.

I finally find her standing right in front of the stage with a group of girls who must be her friends. My blood starts singing in my veins. My eyes caress her from backstage. Her friends' expressions are excited, yet hers is cool as she smiles at them and gives half-hearted nods before she looks all around the stage, lips pursed as she studies everything. She scans the crowd behind her, and my chest clenches. Is she looking for me, the man she met in the bathroom?

Maybe it's an egotistical thought, but I hope she is. My jaw clenches as I imagine her looking for some other man. She didn't mention a boyfriend or date, and

I can't forget how she blushed so prettily under my intense gaze. I've never been as attracted to a woman as I am Melody, and I'm kicking myself for not getting her number. But this is my show, and I have ways of ensuring I get her attention.

A smile tugs at the corner of my mouth as the emcee announces us. The crowd goes wild, jumping and screaming, but I don't see any of them. My eyes are pinned on my little Melody.

She claps politely but not overly enthusiastically. I've never wanted to impress someone so much. I'm praying she'll enjoy our performance as I step out on the stage, determined to give it my all.

My heart leaps the moment our eyes clash. Her pretty brown eyes widen, and her mouth falls open in recognition. I keep my gaze glued to her as my band members key up the number, and I begin stroking my electric guitar.

When I open my mouth and start singing, I stare directly into her beautiful brown eyes.

Melody.

CHAPTER 3

Melody

OH, my god, it's *him*.

Xavier.

I lean over to Lila and ask, although I already know the answer, "What's the lead singer's name?"

"Xavier," she tells me with a dreamy smile. "Isn't he hot?"

I don't answer. Instead, I turn my eyes back to the stage where he's staring at me. My cheeks heat as he seems to sing directly to me. His eyes never waver from mine. He doesn't scan over the crowd. They stay pinned on me, and before I know it, the stares of all the surrounding people flicker to me, including my friends, whose mouths are falling open in shock.

"Is he staring at you?" Lila asks in astonishment.

"Oh, my god, do you know him?" Another one of the girls asks.

"I may have met him earlier," I admit, "when I was looking for the restroom."

Lila's mouth falls open, and she looks betrayed. "How could you not mention you met the lead singer of Fallen Angels? We've been buzzing about them for the past ten minutes, and you never said a word."

"I didn't know who he was," I insist.

All the girls give me incredulous looks like I must be the stupidest bitch on the planet.

"He never told me he was the lead singer," I defend myself.

Lila shakes her head. "Melody, you are so clueless. He probably assumed you knew who he was since you're at *his* concert."

My face colors as I look back up at the stage. Is that what this is? He's getting me back for not knowing who he is? Is he that type of egotistical celebrity? Is he offended I didn't know who he was?

My cheeks grow hot with mortification when I remember I dissed his band to him. I scoffed and made it sound like his music was beneath me—like I was only here because my friends dragged me here, which is true, but still.

My face burns, and I can't breathe. His gaze penetrates me. Those emerald-green eyes are somehow more luminous in the stage lighting. They burn me, searing my soul as I let his music wash over me.

His voice is perfect. It's an alluring combination of tenor and grit. Smooth and rough at the same time. I don't know how he accomplishes that, but it washes over my senses like smooth sandpaper. I know. The analogy doesn't make any sense to me either, but it's the only way I can describe it.

It's an almost erotic experience that has my nipples pebbling under my shirt and a pulse throbbing between my legs.

Xavier's eyes heat as if he can see what he's doing to me. Then, they come to a break in the song. He pulls his gaze from mine long enough to do a solo guitar riff. The crowd goes wild as his shaggy hair hangs in front of his face, his muscular arms flexing as he works the guitar with expertise.

He steps up to the mic. His eyes land on me again as he finishes the song.

Okay, I never thought I cared about today's music, but Xavier Kane is truly talented. His band is amazing. It's hip and fresh, yet I detect influences from classic rock stars. I'd be lying if I said the Fallen Angels haven't gained a new fan, and it's not only because Xavier Kane is the most handsome man ever to walk the planet. I genuinely love their music.

People continue to stare at me over the following three songs as Xavier sings directly into my eyes. I ignore the crowd and let the music wash over me. The lyrics are as beautiful as the music. They speak of love and pain, things easy for everyone to identify with. It's no wonder they're a hit sensation.

I see the triumph in Xavier's eyes. I think me not knowing who he was and having heard none of his songs challenged him, and maybe that's why he's staring at me like this.

My breath hitches. His eyes seem to imply more than that, though. He's looking at me *possessively* like he thinks I'm *his*.

Almost like a *boyfriend* would sing to his *girlfriend*.

I blush at the thought.

I'm aware of the envious stares of Lila and her friends. I suppose this is almost every woman's dream in this audience. These superfans who have a crush on Xavier would kill to have him singing directly to them like this.

Another song ends, and Xavier holds his hands up to still his bandmates before he steps up to the mic and begins speaking instead of singing. "This next one goes out to Melody, the girl I've been singing to all night."

He winks and points at me before the song queues up, and hundreds of pairs of eyes turn on me again. To my mortification, my face flashes on the Jumbotron, so everyone in the freaking arena knows exactly who Xavier Kane has been singing to all night.

I stare at my face on the screen, my heart beating loudly in my ears. "Mortified" is an understatement. I've always been a bit on the shy side. It's bad enough he's been staring at me all night, but now to have everybody know it's me…

To see my face up on the big screen like that…

I don't like being the center of attention like this. I never have.

I look down, my cheeks burning.

My chest gets tight.

My palms get sweaty.

I can't breathe.

Oh, God, no. Not here! Anywhere but here. Anywhere but now with everyone's eyes trained on me.

Mind-numbing fear holds me in its grip. I glance up at Xavier wildly. I see his brow furrow at the no-doubt panicked expression on my face. He takes a step toward the edge of the stage like he's going to come to me, and I can't take it anymore.

I turn on my heels and bolt, pushing my way desperately through the crowd. I need to get out of here before it hits me full force, and my anxiety attack is broadcasted on the big screen in front of all these people.

I haven't had one since I was a preteen, but I still remember their ferociousness. I suppose it was inevitable I would have one now with all this attention on me. That's what caused them in the first place.

I shake my head as I gulp air. I can't think about that now. I must focus on getting out of this crowded room.

I finally make my way to the back of the crowd, and they begin parting for me. Maybe everyone can tell my desperation. I don't know how the crowd is suddenly parting for me, but I'm grateful for small miracles.

I discover why the crowd is parting when a pair of hands grip my shoulders from behind. I gasp and spin to find none other than Xavier Kane towering over me, concern in his eyes.

"What's wrong, Melody?"

I can't speak. All I can do is shake my head and gasp out ragged breaths as I try to tamp down the illogical anxiety. I know somewhere in the back of my mind there's no threat here, but I can't stop the all-encompassing fear seizing me.

Xavier wraps a protective arm around my shoulders and leads me quickly through the crowd. I don't know where he's taking me, and at this point, I'm beyond caring. I huddle into him, keeping my head down and hiding my face from the masses.

Finally, the buzz of the crowd diminishes until there's nothing but silence. Sweet, beautiful silence. I look up and try to find something to focus on. My therapist always told me that helps. Don't think of anything. Find something blue. Find something red. Engage your mind and think of something else. Find something green.

Xavier cups my cheeks, and my eyes shoot up to his green orbs. *Something green, something green*, I chant in my head.

"Breathe, Melody," Xavier encourages. "In." He sucks in a breath, and I follow him. "Out." He nods at me encouragingly while expelling his breath.

I expel my breath.

He takes me through several more motions, breathing in and out, as I stare into his green eyes.

My heart rate begins to settle as I keep my eyes pinned on his and allow him to lead me to calm.

I finally break eye contact with him when I can breathe on my own again. My cheeks flame when I realize I just had an anxiety attack in front of an entire arena full of people. "I'm sorry," I whisper as the tears begin to fall. "I had an anxiety attack."

"No," Xavier says firmly, "I'm the one who's sorry, Melody. I didn't mean to trigger you like that."

I shake my head, but I don't deny it because seeing my face on that Jumbotron was triggering. I wipe at my tears, though I know it's useless. In the aftermath of an anxiety attack, I'm always overly emotional and exhausted. As soon as I wipe the tears away, fresh ones spring up in their place.

"How did you know what was happening?" I ask as I try to get myself under control.

"I used to have anxiety attacks too," he tells me solemnly.

My eyes widen at his confession. "But you do so well on the stage. I would never have guessed."

"Not all anxiety attacks are caused by eyes closing in on you."

"Yes, I know."

"I take it yours was?" He raises an eyebrow at me.

I nod wearily.

"Do you want to talk about it?"

I immediately shake my head no.

"Might help," he prompts.

"You'll think it's silly."

"I swear I won't," he vows. He pauses before he speaks again. "You want to know what caused mine?"

I glance at him.

"Clowns."

"Clowns?" I repeat.

He lets out a breath. "Yeah, those fuckers with the

painted faces and the big red noses. I've been scared of them since I was a little boy. It got so bad that I would have an anxiety attack every time I saw one. I still don't like the fuckers, but I haven't had an attack for years now."

I don't say anything. No words can help with the pain of anxiety attacks, so I offer my silent support.

"I didn't tell you that to try to get you to confide in me," he finally adds. "If you don't want to tell me, that's fine, but you said I would think it's silly. I guarantee I won't. Because you can't get much sillier than mine."

I take a deep breath as I consider. Xavier is a stranger to me, yet him sharing his secret makes me feel safe to do the same. Who knows? He might be right. It might help. I've only ever talked about my anxiety attacks with my shrink.

"When I was eight, my mother was determined to turn me into a model. She signed me up for a fashion show at the mall. It was this silly little thing. I didn't want to do it and begged her not to make me, but she forced me. Made me practice my walk every day after school."

I glance up at Xavier. "I've never been a fan of getting up in front of a bunch of people, but she insisted. I was so nervous when I walked out on stage that my arms and legs were shaking. No matter how hard I tried to still them, it was something I couldn't control."

I take a deep breath before admitting, "I tripped and fell right there in front of hundreds of people. I heard all the other kids laughing at me. I heard their moms trying to hush them, and I sat there frozen on stage, crying until my mother had to come carry me off. I know she was disappointed in me, but she's a good mom." I rush to defend her. "She did her best to make it right. She didn't push me to do stuff like that again, and she enrolled me in therapy. My therapist says that event is what triggered it all, and she helped teach me some coping mechanisms. They tried medication, but I didn't like how it made me spaced out, so we worked on the underlying issues instead. It all went back to that event, and my mom felt terrible about it."

I stare at Xavier's chest as I lose myself in my memories. I remember the therapist explaining the difference between anxiety and panic attacks. The terms are often used interchangeably, but anxiety attacks usually have triggers, whereas panic attacks don't have to have a trigger. Anxiety attacks aren't generally as intense as panic attacks. If panic attacks are more intense than anxiety attacks, I genuinely feel for those with a panic disorder.

"I thought I was over it," I finally admit softly. "I

haven't had an episode since I was fifteen, but—" I stop talking.

"I threw you in the limelight in front of a bunch of people," he answers for me, his lips thinning. "Jesus, Melody, I'm so sorry. I had no idea."

I shake my head. "You couldn't have known, and while we're apologizing, I'm sorry," I tell him, a flush creeping up my face. "I didn't realize that was your dressing room earlier. And I'm sorry I didn't know who you were."

He smiles as he tucks a lock of hair behind my ear. The gesture is so tender it makes me breathless. "Never apologize for being genuine."

"For what it's worth, I thought you guys were great."

His smile widens, and his eyes light with pride. "Yeah?"

"Yeah."

He laughs. "I've just impressed my toughest critic. You have no idea how badly I wanted you to like my music."

"Is that why you were staring at me while you were singing?"

Xavier's eyes trail over my face before they settle on my lips. "I think you know why I was staring at you, Melody."

My breath hitches as Xavier steps closer.

"Breathe," he instructs.

I let out of whoosh of air.

"You should probably get back out there," I say, my voice breathy as his eyes hold me captive.

"It's my show. I can do what I want. Besides, we were done with our set. The other band members can handle it."

"Oh," I say lamely, my breath hitching again at the way Xavier is staring at me so intensely.

"Last name?" he finally asks me.

I blink, surprised by the question. "Martin."

"Melody Martin." He says my name thoughtfully. "I want to see a lot more of you, Melody Martin," he adds right before his lips cover mine.

I forget all about anxiety attacks and rock star performances as his lips slide sensuously over mine in a heart-meltingly perfect kiss. It's a kiss I know will destroy me for all future kisses. At that moment, I know Xavier Kane has the power to wreck me.

CHAPTER 4

Xavier

ONE TASTE of Melody's lips, and I know this girl is the only one I want to kiss for the rest of my life. It should scare me how quickly her lips lock me down, but it doesn't. Instead, it's like a gear slips into place inside me. Something within me clicks, and it feels so right.

More, my body demands. I angle her head and plunder deeper into her mouth, sweeping my tongue against hers. The way she moves her tongue against mine so tentatively sends fire roaring through my veins.

I'd bet my last million that Melody's sweet little

pussy is untapped. I don't have a virgin fetish, but the thought that no other man has ever been inside her drives me mad with the primal urge to claim her as mine before someone else comes along and does it.

This girl is *mine*. There's no denying it. I was drawn to her from the first moment I saw her, and now I've tasted her, I'll be damned if I ever let another man near her.

I spear my fingers into her tresses and moan into her mouth. She whimpers back, a beautiful sound that makes my cock harder than a steel rod. Fuck, I want her.

Before I can control myself, my lips slide over her cheeks and down to her neck, where I lick and suck on the sweet flesh. I inhale deeply, taking in her fresh cherry cola scent. She smells young and innocent. She smells like *mine*.

I suddenly realize I don't even know how old she is. "How old are you, Melody?" I ask between kisses. The breathy little noises she's making are driving me crazy.

"Nineteen," she breathes. "Why?"

"Thank fuck," I groan before I smash my lips onto hers. I don't know what I would have done if she wasn't legal. I can't fight this pull to her.

I don't tell her how old I am. I'm twenty-seven, but she'll find out soon enough if she goes home and does her homework. If she looks up my biography online, it'll all be right there, and it's the smart thing for her to do after getting involved with a rock star like me.

My hands glide over her delicate shoulders and around to cup her breasts. Her nipples pebble under my fingertips through her little blue tube top.

With a growl, I yank the top down to expose those perfect little cherries and fall on them like a hungry beast, sucking one and then the other into my mouth. How does she taste so sweet everywhere?

"Oh my god," Melody whimpers as she spears her fingers through my hair, and I hold her close with my hand splayed on the small of her back as I feast on her breasts. They're perfect. Not too big, not too small. Enough to be a nice little handful.

I slip my hand beneath her denim skirt to cup her ass, hissing in a breath when I discover she's wearing nothing but a thong. The thought that her bare ass cheeks have been so close to being exposed all night has me both achingly aroused and furious.

"I can't decide whether I want to spank your little bottom or worship it," I moan against her skin.

"What?" she asks in a breathy, confused voice.

"What are you doing leaving your house in this mini skirt and a thong? Do you realize any pervert could have seen this sweet ass?" I mold her rounded globes in my hands.

"I didn't think," Melody gasps.

I pull her flush against me and hump my hard cock into her through my jeans. The heat of her pussy brands me through her panties. I move my hand to cup her panty-covered mound. Her heat sears my palm, and I pull her panties to the side to test her wetness with my fingers.

Her hand suddenly grips my wrist, her eyes wide. "Xavier," she says my name hesitantly. "I've never—I—"

A wave of relief washes over me. I know what she's going to say. I suspected, but the confirmation is nice.

She doesn't say it, though. She merely stops and bites her lip.

"You've never?" I prompt her.

She looks away from me as if she's embarrassed.

I gently guide her chin back to me so I can capture her eyes again. "You've never what, beautiful?" I ask her softly. "Say it."

"I've never had sex before," she admits with a charming blush.

I close my eyes. "Thank fuck," I whisper.

When I open my eyes, she's looking at me curiously with her head cocked to the side. "You're happy about that?" She seems confused.

I grin at her. "Hell, yeah, beautiful. Why wouldn't I be?"

"Well, I don't know," she stammers. "You're a rock star, so I'm sure you're used to experienced women."

I frown because her statement is true, and I wish it weren't. I wish I'd saved myself for her like she did me.

"Melody," I say her name firmly. "Knowing I'll be the first man inside you fills me with more joy than I've ever known. I only wish you were my first, too, but I promise you no one could ever compare to you."

Melody looks up at me again. I can see the worry in her eyes. She's nervous. For all I know, she's never done *anything*, and bastard that I am, that pleases me to no end.

The thought I could be her first *everything* has me burning to know the answer. "Was this your first kiss?"

Her cheeks turn pink, and she looks down.

I'm having none of that. I want to look into her eyes when she answers me, so I tilt her chin up to me. "Was it?"

She nods as she confesses softly, "Yes."

Her confirmation fills me with a rush of possessiveness, and I crash my lips to hers, kissing her voraciously. She's panting against my lips when I finally pull back, and my chest heaves with pent-up emotions.

This woman. She's now my everything. I know it's fast, but ask me if I give a fuck.

My hand slides between her legs again, but she grabs it.

"Xavier," she says my name, and my eyes instantly find hers.

God, I love the way my name sounds on her lips. I want to hear her panting it in that breathy, husky little voice when I'm balls deep inside her with her virgin blood on my cock, proving she's mine and only mine.

She bites her lip. My eyes home in on the motion, watching as the flesh turns pink and puffy. "I don't know if I'm ready..."

I withdraw my hand and give her a gentle kiss on the forehead. Although my cock is leaking, I'm not in this for a quick fuck. Melody is my endgame, and I need her to know that. I need her to feel safe with me and know I'll always respect her.

"I'll never pressure you to do anything you're not ready for, beautiful." I gather her against my chest and stroke my hands through her hair soothingly, like I'm petting a frightened kitten. "We can go as slow as you like. We have all the time in the world."

"We do?" she asks hesitantly.

"Yes," I assure her, "because I want to get to know you, everything about you."

Her eyes are wide and incredulous. "You do?" she asks skeptically.

"Yes, I do."

Her brow furrows. "But why? You're the lead singer of the most famous rock band on the planet, and I'm," she shrugs self-deprecatingly, "well, *me.*"

I frown. "Don't do that."

Her eyes widen.

I elaborate, "Don't diminish yourself. You're amazing, Melody. Do you think I call you beautiful for nothing? It's not a line. I'm not some guy trying to get in your pants, and I certainly don't say things I don't mean. If I call you beautiful, it's because I think you are beautiful. And it's more than this pretty brown hair," I finger a silky lock, "and this hot little body you've got. It's *you.* I knew the moment I laid eyes on you, there was something special about you. You were shining with this inner light. It's something I haven't seen very often in my career. When I tell you I want to spend time with you and get to know you better, I mean it. You got that?"

She nods up at me shyly. "Okay. I guess there's no harm in us being friends."

I bark out a laugh. "Make no mistake, Melody," I lean in closer to her lips. "I want to be much more than your friend, but we can start with friends if it makes you comfortable." I'm so close her cherry cola scent fills my nostrils. I leak a steady stream of precum, which slides down my swollen length onto my balls. Fuck, I want her!

She smiles at me, and it's like an arrow of light piercing my heart.

The sound of the crowd chanting my name finally reaches us.

We look at one another.

"You need to get back out there," Melody gently prods me. "You've got a lot of fans counting on you."

I sigh. It's true, and I don't want to disappoint them, but Melody is the only person I care about being around right now.

"Okay," I agree, "but not before I get your number. I'm not letting you slip away from me this time, Melody Martin."

She laughs and hands me her phone.

I quickly program myself in and pull her in for another hug and a lingering kiss before I turn to head back to the stage. "Wait for me here until I get back," I instruct as I reach the door and turn for one last look at her.

She nods and takes a seat on my couch. That satisfies me, but as I return to the stage, all I can think about is pressing Melody into the sofa and feasting on that untapped little pussy.

Melody Martin is *mine*.

CHAPTER 5

Melody

"SO, SPILL," Lila orders me as she plops down on my bed cross-legged and looks at me expectantly.

I shrug. "There's nothing to tell." My smile betrays me.

She slaps my shoulder playfully. "There is too, you whore! Now tell! Starting with how you met Xavier Kane!"

I know Lila won't let up until she gets her way, so I tell her the story about how I had to pee so badly, glaring at her since it was one-hundred percent her fault for refusing to stop because she didn't want to be late getting to the arena. I tell her about how I burst into Xavier's dressing room to use the bathroom.

I blush as I admit, "I can't believe he wants anything to do with me. I know he must have heard me celebrating after I found a toilet."

Lila laughs before she preens proudly. "See? You should be thanking me for not pulling over, or you wouldn't have met Mr. Right."

I look down. "I wouldn't call him that. We're just friends." My heart hammers in my chest when I remember how Xavier kissed me.

Lila scoffs. "Friends don't sing to each other in front of an entire arena full of people with their hearts in their eyes, Melody. Xavier Kane has *never* done that. The guy digs you, and I'm not gonna lie, I'm jealous as hell." She says it playfully, and I know my roommate is truly happy for me.

Lila shakes her head in disbelief and gets a faraway, dreamy look in her eyes. "Do you realize how romantic this is? You have the perfect little meet-cute story to tell your grandchildren."

"Whoa!" I hold up my hands. "Who said anything about children, much less grandchildren?"

Lila waves her hand like it's a detail to be taken care of later.

I didn't tell Lila *everything* that passed between

Xavier and me, although after her pressing, I admitted we'd kissed, but nothing else. She thinks I'm crazy for not sleeping with him.

"What is wrong with you, girl?" she demands. "I can't believe you didn't pounce on that. Any other girl would have."

I look down. I've never told Lila I'm a virgin, and I don't plan on telling her now. It's no one's business but my own—and now Xavier's, I guess. I blush when I remember how Xavier stormed into the dressing room after the final performance and immediately took me in his arms, pressing his lips against mine. The man knows how to kiss a girl senseless. If he keeps kissing me like that and making it so I can't think straight, I won't be a virgin for much longer.

Xavier desires me. The evidence is there. I still can't believe it, but the insanely hot rock star wants *me*. I press my legs together when I remember how that huge, hard part of him pressed into me.

I waited for him like he instructed, and true to his word, he didn't press me to do anything sexual. Instead, he kissed me for what seemed like hours between talking. I don't know how long we sat in his dressing room, but it was long enough for him to order in food. He asked me what I wanted, and when I said cheese pizza, that's exactly what he got.

He hung on my every word like I was the most fascinating thing on the planet. He asked me about my likes and dislikes, my interests, and my childhood. If he could sense I didn't want to talk about something, he didn't press me. He always respected my boundaries like a perfect gentleman.

He asked me what I was majoring in and didn't seem judgmental when I told him I wasn't sure yet, that I was still figuring things out. No, he seemed to understand.

Though he couldn't keep his hands off me, he never went beyond what I allowed, and honestly, there's not much I wouldn't allow at this point. I've known him scarcely a day, and he's completely gained my trust.

I'm either insane or hopelessly naïve, but it is what it is.

"So, come on," Lila prompts me. "What do you think of him? Are you going to see him again? And you better say yes because if you don't, I swear I'll kick you out. You won't be my roommate anymore."

I can't stop the smile that breaks across my face. "Okay, yes, Xavier is amazing, and yes, I am going to see him again."

As if on cue, my cell phone buzzes, and my smile widens as I look down and see a text from Xavier.

My Rock Star: Hey, beautiful. What are you up to?

I laugh when I see the way Xavier programmed

himself into my phone. My heart does a flip when I see he denoted himself as *my* rock star.

I decide to answer honestly.

Me: Talking about you to my roommate.

He hits me back immediately.

My Rock Star: All good, I hope.

Me: Oh, yes. She's one of your biggest fans.

My Rock Star: I hope you are my biggest fan because I'm your biggest fan.

Cue my swooning heart.

"Is it him?" Lila asks with a knowing, shit-eating grin on her face.

I look up at her and nod.

"Oooh, let me see!" She grabs my cell phone from me.

"Hey!" I protest at how quickly she snatches it from me, but I'm not angry. I don't mind her seeing our conversation so far.

"Aw!" she gushes. "So not only is he insanely hot and uber-talented, but he's also sweet and gushy and romantic."

Lila types on my phone, and I panic. There's no telling what she's sending him.

I snatch the phone back. "What the crap are you doing?" I groan at her.

She gives me a smug look, and I see she hit "Send" right before I snatched the phone back.

Me: I'm telling her how amazing you are.

My Rock Star: You think I'm amazing?

My face is burning as I type back.

Me: Sorry. My crazy roommate grabbed my phone.

My phone buzzes instantly.

My Rock Star: So you don't think I'm amazing?

A sad emoji with puppy dog eyes follows the message.

I laugh as I answer.

Me: I didn't say what she said was untrue.

He sends an emoji with hearts for eyes.

My Rock Star: I think you're pretty amazing too, Melody. Which brings me to my question. When can I see your amazing ass?

I smile.

Me: I'm free all weekend.

My Rock Star: I'm free until my show tonight, but I'll cancel it if I can have you all weekend.

Me: No. You can't disappoint your fans.

I can't stop the smile that pulls at my lips at the thought he would do that for me.

My Rock Star: When can I come get you?

Me: When were you thinking?

My Rockstar: How about now?

Me: But I'm not even dressed.

I send a laughing emoji, assuming he's kidding.

My Rock Star: Even better. Open the door. I'm right outside.

I read the text out loud in shock. I look at Lila in panic, but she laughs like a crazed hyena as I bounce over to the closet to find a pair of shorts to put on since I'm currently braless in nothing but a skimpy tank top and panties.

On the other hand, Lila went out earlier, so she's dressed.

Before I have a chance to throw on a pair of shorts, I hear her open the door, and then Xavier is standing right there with his intense green gaze fixed on me.

I glare at my traitorous roommate. "Bitch," I mouth at her.

But she's beaming between us as she grabs her purse and looks at the imaginary watch on her wrist. "Oh, would you look at the time? I have somewhere to be. You two have fun!" She winks at me dramatically. "Oh, and awesome show last night, Xavier," she says when she gets to the door.

"Thank you, doll," he says with a wink and a smile before she closes the door behind her.

Xavier's gaze instantly returns to me and rakes over my nearly naked form. "If I knew this is how you would greet me, I would have come in sooner."

"How did you get here so fast?" I ask him.

"I've been sitting outside for over an hour," he tells me frankly.

I laugh, thinking he's kidding, but when I glance at him, his expression is serious. "You're kidding, right?" My eyes widen as I look at him. I see no humor in his gaze. He's telling the truth.

Xavier shrugs. "I told you I don't say things I don't mean."

My brow furrows. "Why did you do that?"

"Because I couldn't stay away any longer," he admits, closing the distance between us and pulling me flush against his chest.

He makes no move to kiss me, just holds me close. His chest expands as he inhales me in a gesture more intimate than if he'd placed his lips on mine. The tremble that ripples through him echoes in my body. It's crazy. He's so big, and I'm so tiny, yet we somehow fit together.

As if he's inside my head, he mirrors my thoughts. "See how well we fit together, Melody?"

My throat is tight, and I can't speak, so I nod against his chest.

"God, what are you doing to me, Melody? I can't breathe without you, beautiful." He tips my head up to his. His green eyes bore into mine as he lowers his lips and kisses me gently. His kiss is so tender that tears spring to my eyes.

He pulls back and gently wipes away the tears escaping down my cheeks. "Don't cry, beautiful. I promise I'm not one of those psycho stalkers, but I won't lie. I'm becoming more obsessed with you by the minute."

Those words probably shouldn't send a rush of warmth through me, but they do. They're like a balm to my insecure heart. I've never been very confident.

I laugh, and he cups my cheek. "There, that's better. I love to see you smile, Melody."

I sober as the air between us thickens. He stares at my lips for a long moment, and his eyes return to mine. I stare at him, knowing what he wants. He's assured me he won't press me before I'm ready, but an answering throb pulses deep in my core.

I look down and lick my lips, considering. What am I waiting for? I'm nineteen years old and haven't lost my V-card yet because I've never met anyone I could imagine giving myself to in that way. As I look at Xavier, something within me falls into place. He's the only one I want to share this experience with.

Xavier is completely still as he watches me. My heart thunders in my chest as I stand on my tiptoes and press my lips softly against his. He stays still, letting me take the lead, and I'm thankful for that. I wrap my arms around his neck and pull him down to me. He comes willingly, and when I slip my tongue against his lips, he immediately opens for me and lets me slide in to tangle with his.

Once my tongue twines with his, something inside Xavier snaps, and he grabs my face with both hands and kisses me back voraciously. My heart thumps so loudly that I can hear it in my head as liquid pools between my thighs. I move my hand between us and cup his hardness through his pants. He groans into my mouth and thrusts into my hand. My eyes widen when I realize how big he is there. He thrust against my panties yesterday, so I already knew he was well-endowed, but now that I'm feeling him with my hand, I realize he's so big that my palm doesn't even halfway cover him.

Xavier pulls back to look into my eyes searchingly. "Are you sure about this, Melody? We don't have to do anything if you're not ready."

My heart melts at his reassurance. I know he means it. It must physically hurt him to be that hard and not get any relief, but despite how much he wants me, he would wait.

With that knowledge bolstering me, I take a deep breath and answer him. "Yes, I'm sure. I want you, Xavier. Take me."

I don't have to tell him twice. With a growl, he picks me up with both hands cupped under my ass. I wrap my arms and legs around him as that hot, pulsing part of him settles right against my core. He kisses me while he humps against me, and I stop thinking. I surrender to the sensations and submit to him, trusting him to take care of me.

I know he will.

I trust him.

CHAPTER 6

Xavier

I FEEL the moment Melody submits to me. She's soft and pliant in my arms, and her trust is the most amazing gift anyone has ever given me. It humbles me so much that tears damn near spring to my eyes.

"God, look at you, beautiful," I whisper to her in between kisses. "So perfect for me. I'm going to keep you forever. You know that, don't you, Melody? You're mine, sweet baby. *Mine.*" My voice turns growly the more I speak, but I can't help it. She's bringing out the animal in me.

She makes a mewling sound that goes straight to my heart—and my cock. I carry her to her bed and lay her gently down upon it. I graze my lips over every exposed inch of her delectable skin. I want to kiss every bit of her, *taste* every part of her.

She trembles under my lips, especially when I reach her panties and peel them from her body. The scent of her arousal assaults me, and my mouth salivates in response. I've never wanted to taste someone as badly as I do Melody.

And Jesus, Mary, and Joseph, that first lick is like heaven. Tangy sweetness explodes on my tongue, and I know I want to taste this pussy every day for the rest of my life.

Melody cries out, her legs closing around my head, but I hold her thighs open. She's shaking underneath me. Her hands fist in my hair, and she half pulls, half pushes me away.

I look up at her flushed complexion as I feast on her sweetness. She's panting and writhing in pleasure, and I swear I've never seen a more beautiful sight. I can't wait to see what she looks like when she comes all over my cock.

Her fingers tighten painfully in my hair when I press a probing finger into her. Her breath catches, and she looks down at me with wild eyes. Her tight pussy clenches around my finger, and that clench registers in my cock. I groan as a jet of precum shoots from my tip to stain the inside of my boxers. Fuck, if I keep this up, I'm going to nut in my pants like a horny fratboy.

"Fuck, Melody, you're so tight," I growl between licks.

She makes a strangled noise as I suction onto her clit, hollowing my cheeks and batting my tongue back and forth over it.

"Oh god!" she cries out as her back arches off the bed. "Xavier!"

I continue to suck on her hard while I gently thrust my finger in and out of her. When I add a second finger inside her and curl my fingers up to find the spongy spot on the inner wall of her pussy, she screams out my name, her entire body bowing.

"Yes, that's it, sweet baby," I encourage as I continue to rub circles around her g-spot. "Come for me."

She's damn near sobbing as her muscles contract around my fingers, and her juices gush out onto my hand.

I growl as I lick up all her sweet cream. Her body jerks every time my tongue sweeps across her swollen clit.

"Fuck, I can't wait anymore," I tell her as I scramble on top of her and release my aching length from the confines of its prison. I groan in relief as my cock bobs free between us, the fucker so hard and swollen it's pointing straight up to my belly button.

I see Melody's eyes widen as she takes in my erection. She bites her lip, a look of worry on her face. I get it. I'm big everywhere and very well-endowed.

"Hey," I say softly, and her eyes flick back to me. "I promise I'll try my best not to hurt you. It might hurt a bit the first time," I tell her honestly, "but I'll do everything I can to make it better after that first pinch of pain."

She nods and smiles at me. "I know," she says in that soft, husky little voice. "I trust you, Xavier."

My chest tightens with emotion as I cup her cheeks and kiss her, trying to communicate everything I'm feeling with the kiss.

She softens underneath me, and I take the opportunity to press myself slowly into her.

She gasps into my mouth as the crown pops in, and I still, my entire body straining with the effort not to surge forward and tear through her innocence.

"Are you okay?" I ask her, my voice strained.

"Yes," she nods. "You're so big."

"That's not even a fourth of what I have to give you, baby."

Her eyes widen as I feed more of my length into her. I watch her lashes flutter as she whimpers. Sweat beads on my brow as I keep pushing into her slowly until her hymen greets the tip of my cock.

Her eyes flutter open, and she smiles at me. "That wasn't so bad," she admits.

Her smile is so damn beautiful it takes my breath away every time I see it. "We're only halfway there, sweet girl," I warn her.

Her eyes widen again. "There's more?"

I grit my teeth as her sweet pussy pulses around me. "I haven't pushed through your hymen yet."

"Oh," she says as she looks up at me with wide eyes, "but I'm already so full."

"Well, I'm about to fill you to the brim, beautiful. Are you ready?"

She hesitates slightly before she nods her head.

That's all the consent I need. I thrust up into her, tearing her innocence to shreds until I'm fully sheathed inside the tightest, wettest pussy I've ever experienced.

She cries out and clings to me, and my heart thunders in my chest in victory. "Mine," I groan. "Fuck, Melody, you feel that? You're mine, sweet baby."

My girl clings to me, and a surge of protectiveness wells up deep inside me. This woman is *mine*. Mine to love. Mine to fuck. Mine to protect.

I drop kisses on her forehead, her eyes, her cheeks, her lips. My tenderness for this girl has me tied up in knots. My body demands that I move, but I have to ensure she's okay first.

"Melody?"

She opens her chocolate brown eyes and focuses them on me.

"Are you okay, beautiful?"

I see the way her features soften at my words. "Yes," she finally whispers. "It doesn't hurt anymore."

She lifts her hips against me, and I hiss in a breath as the movement causes me to slide inside her tight channel.

She moans too. "Feels so good now," she murmurs.

"It's about to feel even better, sweet baby," I tell her as I start to stroke my full length in and out of her, studying her face to watch every expression: surprise, wonder, pleasure.

Fuuuck. The little sounds she makes and the look on her face is enough to get me off in record time. The base of my spine tingles. My heavy balls draw up and grow tighter.

I reach between us and pet her clit while I grit my teeth, holding back. I *will not* come without her. I don't care if it kills me.

"Fuck, I need you to come for me, Melody," I beg her desperately. I already feel my cum rushing up my stalk. My muscles ache as I try to hold it back, even as I feel it surging to the tip.

"Fuck, Melody!" I groan as I lose the battle, and my release surges violently from the head of my cock as Melody screams and her pussy falls open around me.

I stop fighting it and roar as the second rush comes jetting out of me. Her pussy flutters wildly around me, milking me like a fist, coaxing more cum from me than I thought my balls could carry.

"Oh, fuck, baby, fuck!" I'm almost delirious with pleasure. I keep my wits about me enough to flip us so she's on top of me as I fall onto the bed, completely spent.

Melody is limp in my arms. My half-hard cock is still buried inside her as I stroke my hands over her body. My precious girl. *My* Melody. My chest swells. If I could live permanently connected to her like this, I would.

She nuzzles her head into my neck, and I kiss her forehead tenderly, knowing there's not a damn thing I wouldn't do for this woman.

She's *mine*.

CHAPTER 7

Melody

I SMILE as I look at my phone. A text from Xavier just came through, and it's the same one he sends me before every performance.

My Rock Star: Are you going to be waiting for me backstage like a good girl?

Me: Aren't I always?

My Rock Star: Good. That's the only way I can bear to be parted from you.

I smile. How does it feel to have a man like Xavier Kane telling me the only thing that gets him through a show is knowing I'll be waiting backstage for him? Not gonna lie, it's pretty freakin' amazing.

A pulse throbs between my legs when I think about how he greets me when he comes off the stage every night. He comes bursting into the dressing room and doesn't speak until he's had his lips on me and thoroughly reminded me how much he missed me.

Sometimes he takes me against the wall with my arms or legs wrapped around him. Sometimes he takes me from behind with my front pressed against the wall. Sometimes he puts my knees on the couch and has me hold onto the back of it as he drives into me deep from behind.

I don't know what my favorite position is because Xavier is big no matter how I take him, but he somehow feels even bigger from behind. No sooner does he stuff himself inside me than I'm coming around him while he looks adoringly into my eyes.

Not a day goes by without him tasting me, either. I flush when I recall how voraciously he eats me out, but I understand because I want to taste him just as much. There's something so thrilling about having a huge, powerful man reduced to jelly under the ministrations of my tongue. When I tasted him for the first time, I instantly fell in love with his musky, manly taste. I love knowing I'm driving him crazy. I love how he fists his hands in my hair when he eventually snaps and pumps the rigid column of his flesh down my throat until he explodes in my mouth.

So yeah, if giving him a blowjob is anything like how it feels when he kisses me between my legs, I get why he's so obsessed with it.

He doesn't let me give him blowjobs often, though, claiming he can't take the pleasure of my mouth. It has him coming in no time, and he always wants to come inside my pussy. He says feeling me come while he comes inside me is the best part. Coming together is more than a physical joining. It's a spiritual thing. Our souls are tethered whenever he's deep inside me, staring into my eyes lovingly as he pumps everything he has to give into me.

Since the day Xavier took my virginity, we've been almost inseparable. When he's not setting up or performing, he's glued to me. He's practically moved me into his flat with my textbooks so I can study during the day between him fucking me. He gets my friends free tickets to any concerts they want, and I'm always waiting backstage for him. There's something so thrilling about watching my rock star perform from backstage, knowing he'll be running straight to me as soon as he gets off the stage.

He knows I don't like to be in the limelight, so we keep our relationship under wraps. I can't say I'm thrilled to be a secret girlfriend, but it's at my behest—not his. If it were up to Xavier, he would announce us to the entire world and spend every night singing directly into my eyes with me in the front row. Those are his words—not mine.

Xavier truly is amazing. When we're not together, he's constantly texting and calling to check up on me. Anything I need, he does his best to get for me. He insists we sleep together every night, either at my dorm or his flat. I've gotten so used to having his arms and legs banded around me that I seriously doubt I could sleep alone anymore.

If I have class the next morning, we usually sleep in my dorm, but sometimes he'll insist on sleeping in his flat and driving me to class. I know it bothers him when I ask him to stay in the car when he drops me off. He's a gentleman who wants to walk me to the door, but I know how the college coeds would react if they saw him dropping me off. My palms get sweaty thinking about it. Everyone on campus would have their attention on me, and I hate being in the spotlight—especially after my most recent anxiety attack. I'm terrified of having another one.

I chew on my lip as I consider where this is going. Xavier claims he wants to be with me forever, that he's never letting me go. While those proclamations send a rush of warmth through me, my practical side wonders how this will work. Can I stay in the shadows as his hidden girlfriend forever? Will he be content with that?

Xavier is famous. Whoever is with him needs to be comfortable in the spotlight, and I'm not.

It's not the first time I've worried about things like this concerning our relationship. As amazing as Xavier is, I worry about the practicality of us and how long we can last as a couple with the parameters I've put into place.

My worries are validated when I show up at the venue where Xavier's performing tonight. I try to slip unseen through the backstage door—as he always instructs me—when suddenly cameras are flashing in my face.

I gasp and spin around to find at least ten microphones shoved toward me as the paparazzi scream questions at me.

Where did they come from? It's like they materialized out of thin air.

"Melody, is it true you've secretly been seeing Xavier Kane?"

"How soon did you two meet before he sang to you in front of a crowd?"

"What's your story? How did you meet him?"

"Are you his girlfriend or a groupie?"

I shield my eyes from the flashes as the telltale signs of an impending anxiety attack crash in on me. My palms are sweaty. My breathing is labored. My arms and legs begin to shake. My heart thumps in my chest. My lungs tighten. Oh god, I can't breathe.

Suddenly, the stage door is thrown open, and Xavier's tall form is towering in the doorway. His eyes glitter with anger at the paparazzi as he snaps at them, "Back the fuck off!"

He wraps a protective arm around me, and I bury my head against his chest as he ushers me inside. My chest is tight, and I gulp in huge breaths.

As soon as the door thuds closed behind us, Xavier bends so his face is directly in front of mine. He cups my cheeks and orders me to look at him. "Eyes on me, Melody. Good girl. Breathe in. Breathe out. In. Out."

He leads me through the motions until my heart rate settles and I'm breathing normally. I slump against him, shaken and exhausted, both physically and emotionally.

He gathers me against his chest and presses kisses on my head. "I'm so sorry, beautiful. I didn't mean to let them maul you like that. I'm sorry I wasn't there to fend them off. Fuck, Melody."

"How did they find out?"

Xavier's brow furrows. "I don't know, Melody. I haven't told anyone, but people are always watching me. No doubt the fans have noticed how I rush back-stage after every show, and people are still talking about that night."

He looks at me tenderly. He's talking about the night he sang to me in front of everyone. It's a bitter-sweet memory because it's the night we met, but it's also the night I started having anxiety attacks again after four years.

Of course, I don't blame Xavier for them, though I know he blames himself. I probably didn't have any before then because I always ensure I'm never the center of attention. Now I think back on it, my attacks stopped when I was fifteen—which was when I drew into myself and made sure never to stand out too much.

When I got to college, I mostly stuck to myself, but my stubborn, fun-loving roommate worked on breaking me out of my shell. She talked me into going out more and look at what happened.

I've fallen in love with a rock star. Tears spring to my eyes when the hopelessness of the situation crashes down on me.

I'm in love with Xavier, but I'm a mess around him when the limelight is shifted to me. He's famous and has a lot of fans, so it's not fair to expect him to keep himself or his relationship out of the spotlight for me.

"Xavier, I don't know if—"

Xavier's eyes take on a panicked look, and he smashes his lips onto mine to shush me. He kisses me deeply, desperately, and I instinctively melt into him.

God, the man can kiss me into submission every time.

"Don't you dare," he whispers against my lips. "Don't say it, Melody. We'll make this work. I'll take care of the paps."

He grabs my hand and presses it against his chest, holding it over his heart. "You feel this? My heart beats only for you. We're meant to be. I know you feel it too. Don't bail on me now. We'll get through this together, beautiful. I'll do whatever it takes to protect you."

I nod, my throat tight. I try to blink away the tears that threaten to fall, but one falls anyway.

"Fuck," Xavier curses as he wipes it away, his expression torn. "I'm going to cancel the show, beautiful. I'll take you home, and everything will be okay."

I shake my head adamantly. "No! You can't do that, Xavier. You've got a lot of people counting on you. Don't worry about me. I'll be fine." I give him a brave smile.

He runs a hand through his raven locks and looks at me skeptically. He shakes his head. "No, Melody. You're more important. Let me take you—"

"Xavier!" I interrupt him by cupping his cheeks with my hands. "It's okay. Go out on that stage and be amazing. You've already helped me all you can. I'm okay now. I promise."

It's a lie. I'm not okay. My heart is breaking because I already know what I have to do.

Xavier searches my eyes before he hauls me against his chest and kisses me desperately. I kiss him back just as desperately, trying to memorize the glide of his lips over mine, the way his fingers tangle in my hair, the scent of him.

His chest puffs out, and I know he's inhaling me as deeply as I am him. "You'll be waiting here for me when I come off stage?"

I can't meet his eyes as I lie to him, so I bury my face against his neck and nod.

With one last tender kiss on my forehead, Xavier heads onto the stage.

I stand there with tears streaming down my face as I watch my rock star step back into the limelight where he belongs and where I don't.

CHAPTER 8

Xavier

I HAVE a bad feeling in the pit of my stomach as I exit the stage. That's why I'm not completely surprised to find Melody gone. I felt it in the turning of my gut. I almost walked off the stage twice and wish I'd listened to my intuition. *Always go with your gut.* It's never failed me yet. The one time I should have listened to it, I didn't, and now my girl is gone.

I find my phone and send her a text.

Me: Where are you?

Me: Are you okay?

Me: Let me come get you.

No sooner do I send off those rapid-fire texts does

my phone start blowing up with notifications.

I click on one of them, the anger bubbling up inside me as a clip of the paparazzi peppering Melody with questions before I got outside flashes across the screen. I see the wild look in her eyes. I see her windpipe closing up, and I can practically see the individual hairs on her head shaking as she spirals into the beginnings of an anxiety attack right in front of them, yet the assholes never let up. If anything, they only become more insistent.

My nostrils flare, and I clutch my phone so tightly I'm surprised I don't break the fucker in two. All they care about is the next story. They don't care about the people they assault.

I close my eyes. My Melody. My sweet Melody.

I can deal with the paparazzi's shit. I always joke it off, and I've been trained to deal with them, but Melody hasn't.

I harden my jaw. They've messed with the wrong girl.

Concern for her tightens my chest, and I call her instead of texting her. The phone rings and rings and rings before it goes to voicemail. I immediately call her again. This time it goes straight to voicemail.

I clench my jaw as I call her again.

Again, it goes straight to voicemail.

My phone buzzes with an incoming text, and my

heart falls into my stomach when I read the text from my girl.

My girl: Please don't be mad at me. It's better this way. I can't do this anymore. You're free now. I don't want to hold you back.

"What the fuck?" I roar into the empty room. "I don't want to be fucking free! I want you, Melody!" I don't know who I'm talking to. Myself, the empty room. Maybe I'm just screaming my frustration out into the universe hoping that somehow my words will translate to my girl, that she'll feel my pain and come back to me.

I text her back.

Me: Don't do this, Melody. Please.

I know I sound desperate, but I am. I'll plead and beg and do whatever I have to do to keep my girl, my life, my everything.

I get an error message. I try to send it again, and the message comes back unsent yet again.

My heart feels like someone is squeezing it between their hands.

Melody's message couldn't be any clearer. She's breaking things off with me, and it's all because of those fucking assholes outside.

I grab the nearest thing to me—my electric guitar—and roar as I smash it against the wall over and over again. My chest is heaving by the time I'm done, but

I'm nowhere near spent, and breaking my guitar into a thousand tiny pieces hasn't helped abate the storm inside me. No, it's only stoked it.

I don't intend to take this lying down. I know what Melody and I have is real. I know my girl wants me as badly as I want her. I've got to get her back in my arms and make her see.

I stomp toward the door, my only thought to get to Melody and make her see, beg her if I have to. I'll put my life in her hands. Whatever it takes because I refuse to let this be the end of the best thing that's ever happened to me. I don't give a fuck about my music. None of it matters without her. Without my Melody, my song is dead. She's the muse I never knew I had. Everything I've ever sung, I was singing in anticipation of her. And now I've met her, she's the only thing that inspires me. My life is over without her.

When I exit the stage door and am assaulted by the same paparazzi who closed in on my little Melody earlier, I snap. I fucking *snap.*

I grab the man closest to me and lift him clean off his feet by the scruff of his collar. His eyes go wide right before I land the first punch.

The rest of the paparazzi scatter, and I'm pulling back my hand to land the second punch when I'm suddenly yanked off the guy by my fellow bandmates. They're screaming at me to calm down, asking me what I'm doing, but I'm beyond all that. Somewhere in the distance, I hear police sirens, and the next thing I know, I'm in handcuffs.

As they haul my ass to jail, all I can think about is Melody and how I need to get to her. My heart thumps her name over and over again. *Melody. Melody.*

"Fuck!" I roar.

Melody

My hands fly to my mouth as I watch the clip of Xavier punching the paparazzo who accosted me. His fellow bandmates are on him in a flash, holding him back.

Xavier's face is contorted with rage. This happened only minutes after I texted him it was over. I turned off my phone so I wouldn't see any more texts or calls from him. It went against everything in me not to answer Xavier when he texted and called, but I was doing what I thought was best.

The clip disappears from the screen, and there's live footage of all the paparazzi and news reporters standing outside the jailhouse where Xavier is currently being held. They're speculating on how he probably won't be held for long. They tell what his bail is and how his attorney is assuring everyone he'll be out in no time.

Loyal fans are protesting his arrest on the street, claiming it's all the paparazzi's fault for getting him worked up, but tears sting my eyes as I know that wasn't the cause.

It was *me*. I'm the one who reduced him to this. Me and my irrational fears.

The news anchor reports that he smashed his guitar and he's giving up music. My heart twists within me. I sniffle and wipe my eyes as I stare at the screen.

I can't let him do this. Xavier is genuinely talented. I can't let him throw his passion away because of me.

I look back at the TV screen, taking in all the fans and reporters waiting outside for Xavier to be released. My heart beats wildly as I realize what I have to do.

If I truly care about Xavier, I'll be there for him when he needs me most. This is my fault. He went to jail because of me. The least I can do is overcome my fears and be there for him when he gets out.

While my mind balks at the idea of all those eyes on me, my heart will explode if I don't do something. Before I can chicken out like the coward I am, I head out the door and hail a taxi.

"Where to?" the driver asks.

I swallow hard before I answer. "The county jail."

CHAPTER 9

Xavier

I SCOWL as I walk out of the courthouse. Reporters hold microphones out to me, but I notice they all keep a safe distance, no doubt afraid I'll give them the same shiner I gave their cohort earlier.

I smirk at them and answer their questions with "fuck you," "who gives a fuck?" and "I'm quitting the business."

I hear the collective gasp from all the fans gathered around the courthouse, but I don't give a fuck. I've lost the only thing that matters to me.

"No, you're not," a melodious little voice speaks out strongly yet softly.

All eyes, including mine, turn to her, and my chest tightens at the sight of her. Her face is pale, and her brown eyes are big. Her dark lashes frame them, and I see the twin spots of red staining her cheeks. Her beautiful brown hair tumbles around her shoulders. She looks so tiny, so fragile, yet something in her eyes is fierce and determined.

"Melody,' I croak her name and hurry over, needing to touch her. I take her hands and press them against my chest, my concern for her overriding everything else. "Are you okay, beautiful? What are you doing here? Do you need me to get you away from here?"

I scan her from head to toe. Her body trembles slightly, but her breathing is normal. She's not spiraling into an attack—yet.

Melody holds my gaze and swallows as she shakes her head. "I'm fine, Xavier, but you're not quitting music. You can't. It's part of you—the most important part of you."

I shake my head and adamantly deny her claim, "No, it's not, Melody. Maybe that was true at one time, but not anymore. It's *you*. *You're* the most important part of me. If I have to give all this up, all the fame and the limelight and the bullshit, to be with you, that's what I'll do.

Melody bites her lip and shakes her head. "I can't ask you to do that for me."

"You're not asking me. I'm offering."

"Look at me, Xavier," she tells me. My eyes find hers again, and I notice a new peace in them. "I'm okay," she assures me.

My eyes search over her carefully again. Yes, there's the slight tremble, but Melody is holding her own. She's not having an attack despite us being in the middle of this huge crowd with all these eyes on us.

"For so long, I hid in the shadows," Melody whispers. "I haven't had an attack since I was fifteen because I stopped living then. I did everything I could not to put myself in situations that would trigger one instead of working on dealing with them, and that's no way to live."

She squeezes my hands, and my heart goes out to her, my brave girl. "This is my battle to fight, Xavier, and I'm grateful to you for helping me through it, but I can't hide from the world any longer and hope it goes away. I have to learn how to deal with this on my own."

"You're doing wonderful, beautiful," I praise her, proud as hell of her for coming out here like this. I don't dare to hope what it might mean.

She smiles at me, that beautiful, radiant smile before she adds, "I finally had something worth overcoming my fears for."

My heart takes flight in my chest as hope blossoms within me. "Yeah?"

She lets out a little laugh. "Yeah."

I settle my hands on her waist. "And what is it?" My eyes drink her in, every pretty blush and tremble.

She grins at me. "Are you going to make me say it?"

"Hell, yes, I am," I tell her as a grin breaks out across my face.

"You, Xavier. Being with you is more important to me than hiding from my fears."

My chest is going to explode. That's how much joy and relief her words give me. I pull her flush against me, wrapping my arms around her and holding her close as I look down at her and ask, "Does that mean I can officially tell everyone you're my fiancée?"

Her eyebrows shoot up to her hairline. "Fiancée?"

I nod. "You already know it, Melody. You're the only woman I want for the rest of my life. I'd like to go ahead and introduce you as my wife, but as I don't have a ring on your finger yet, fiancée is the next best thing."

"Aren't fiancées supposed to have rings too?" she teases me.

I lift her left hand to my lips and kiss her ring finger reverently. "We'll go pick you out the biggest one you want as soon as we leave here," I promise her.

Melody laughs again, tears glistening in her eyes. I tenderly stroke my thumb over her cheek, my heart about to burst. I'll never get enough of this woman. My Melody. "Is that a yes?"

She laughs again and buries her face in my neck. I love how she clings to me and nods into my chest. "Yes," she breathes.

My smile is wide as I scream to the crowd, "Everyone, I'm in love with Melody Martin, my fiancée!"

Melody's cheeks are flushed, but it's with pleasure and not fear. I'm so fucking proud of her. Proud of her for trying to overcome her fears. Proud to call her mine.

And there's no way I can keep from kissing her right now, so as the crowd's applause surrounds us, I press my lips against hers and become engulfed in the sweet melody of our lips sliding against one another.

The only music I want to make for the rest of my life is the music I'll make with her.

EPILOGUE

Four Years Later

Melody

I SMILE as I watch Xavier showing our son how to hold his child-sized electric guitar. Cory takes after his father. He's only three, but he already has great musical aptitude. When Xavier and I noticed the melodic tunes he plucked out on his toy guitar, Xavier took it upon himself to buy his son the real thing and began teaching him right away.

Cory's little tongue pokes out of the side of his

mouth, something he always does when he's concentrating. Seeing Xavier working with our son always melts my heart.

There's nothing more important to me than my boys.

It's Saturday, so I'm not at the office. I got pregnant shortly after marrying Xavier, and it's no wonder. Xavier fucked me three ways to Sunday every day, and we've never used protection. We got married a week after Xavier announced to the world that we were engaged, so who knows? I could have been pregnant when I said, "I do."

Despite having a family, I still finished college and finally settled on what I wanted to do with my life. I ultimately became a psychiatrist. I wanted to help others who struggle with the same anxiety issues I do.

I haven't had an anxiety attack since before I married Xavier. I finally learned how to overcome my fears, and I've got plenty of coping strategies if I ever have one again.

It breaks my heart to see how many others struggle with the same issues, but I like knowing I can help them in some small way. It's always gratifying to see the relief lighting my patients' eyes when I explain there's nothing wrong with them and not to be disappointed in themselves if they keep having them after addressing any underlying issues.

The simple fact is that some people are lucky enough to overcome their underlying fears and not have them anymore, and some people will continue to struggle despite doing all the right things. Anxiety disorders are unpredictable, and it helps when they know I struggle with one myself, so I understand where they're coming from. I'm not a therapist who treats them as another case. I've walked in their shoes, and they can sense that.

"Hey, look at our little man," the drummer of Xavier's band says with a huge smile as he walks in the door.

Nash has become Cory's designated babysitter when Xavier and I need some alone time. Who would have thought the gruff, bearded, burly-looking drummer would have a soft spot for children? But it's true. Nash adores our son, and Cory loves him too.

Cory bolts over to Nash and jumps into his arms. Nash laughs and ruffles his hair.

Xavier and I kiss Cory on the forehead, but he's no longer paying attention to us. He's all about Nash.

"You guys have fun and stay out as late as you want. Me and the little guy got this."

"I know you do." I smile at Nash gratefully as Xavier takes my hand and leads me out of the house.

"So, where are you taking me tonight, husband?" I ask Xavier playfully.

He grins at me. His dark hair hangs around his face like it was the day I met him. He still dresses like the hot rock star he is. His band did a tour when I was pregnant, and Xavier insisted I come with him. There was no way he was leaving me behind. He wouldn't be separated from me for even a day, so I did my classes online on the road. It was a special time in our lives, but once Cory came, Xavier refused to tour anymore. Instead, his band performs in and around the city so we can give Cory a stable home life and I can have my career helping people.

Because I spend as much time with Cory as I can, I rarely get to wait backstage for Xavier after performances, so when we pull up to the arena he's been performing at all week, I give him an inquisitive look.

"I didn't think you were performing tonight?" My heart sinks at the thought of sharing him. I want my rock star all to myself tonight.

"Oh, I'm performing, beautiful." He gives me that heart-stopping handsome grin. "But it's for an audience of one."

I get his meaning as he pulls me into the building and onto the empty stage where the band's equipment is set up.

Xavier doesn't even grab a mic. He places his hands on my waist and looks into my eyes as he sings to me. He sings the love song he wrote especially for me. The first time I heard it was when he sang it at our wedding. Suffice it to say, I was a blubbering mess, and tears prick my eyes now. My husband singing to me while staring into my eyes like I'm the most precious thing in his world is enough to turn me into a pile of goo at his feet.

As the last note of the song dies away, Xavier cups my face in his hands. "Fuck, Melody, how do you get more beautiful every day?"

"I was going to ask you the same thing."

His smile widens as he pulls me flush against him. His hardness presses into my stomach.

"I think that performance deserves a standing ovation," I say coyly as I drop to my knees in front of him and unzip his pants.

"Melody," he groans as I pull his heavy length from his jeans and kiss the head that's beaded with moisture.

I take my time licking him slowly and teasing him while he jerks against my tongue. I have him so on edge that when I blow lightly on his tip, a jet of precum shoots out and lands on my face.

He growls and hauls me to my feet before his mouth crashes onto mine. "Do you enjoy driving your husband crazy?" he asks me between feral kisses.

"Maybe," I breathe against his neck as his hands slip underneath my dress. He pushes my panties to the side and slides two fingers into me, pumping slowly. "Oh, god," I moan as my head falls back.

His lips latch onto my neck, and he begins to suck rhythmically. I'm going to have a mark, but I don't care. It feels too good.

Xavier kisses all over my body as he lowers me to the stage floor and spreads his huge body atop mine. He hovers over me as he pulls my dress from my body and kisses my nipples. I arch up into him, my pussy aching for him.

As always, my rock star anticipates my needs. The next thing I know, his cock is prodding against my entrance, and then he's filling me completely, deliciously, in a way only he can.

"Still as tight as the day I popped your little cherry," he hisses in my ear as he begins to pump his hips against me frantically.

I'm as desperate as he is, throwing my hips up at him.

"Yes, that's a good girl. Throw that pussy up at me, sweet baby. Give it all to me. You want me to get you pregnant again?"

My pussy clenches at his dirty words before I can answer.

Xavier groans. "Is that a yes? Does my sweet baby want her man to breed her?"

Xavier's breathing becomes more ragged, and he

swells deep inside me. It turns us on when he talks about breeding me, and Cory has been wanting a baby brother or sister.

"Yes, Xavier!" I moan. "Breed me!"

Those words are what does it. Xavier's breath stutters before he goes still and lets out a choked shout as I shatter around him. I scream and cling to him as my orgasm hits me hard. His hot seed spills inside me as I spasm around him uncontrollably.

"Fuck, Melody, take it, baby," he encourages me, sending more ripples straight into my pussy. Every time Xavier jerks inside me, more of his hot liquid bathes my walls.

Xavier keeps himself lodged inside me as he rolls onto his back on the stage with me lying on his chest. "If you don't get pregnant after that, it'll be a miracle. It feels like I had a month's worth of cum stored up for you, baby."

I laugh because the thought of Xavier going a month without release is hilarious. Not a day goes by when he doesn't fuck me, and I'm not complaining. In fact, he's half-hard again already.

"I guess that means you're completely drained and not up for round two," I tease him as I start to wiggle off him.

His arms tighten around me to keep me pinned atop him, and he grins at me. "Uh-uh. You're not going anywhere. I've got a standing ovation for you now."

I grin as I press my lips against his. Xavier's hand finds the nape of my neck as he kisses me deeply, communicating his desire with his lips.

When it comes to my rock star, I'll always have nothing but standing ovations.

Read the rest of the ROCK MY WORLD series!

Your favorite steamy romance authors are giving you a peek into the lives of fourteen sexy couples who will Rock Your World. Wicked talented, sometimes flawed, and too naughty for their own good, our larger-than-life rock stars know how to show their fans a good time. Music and romance go hand-in-hand, and love comes easy…but will it stay? Grab your backstage pass and watch true love tame the wildest hearts around.

Get the entire series here: https://amzn.to/3J26s4E

Connect with Emma!

Visit Emma's website to get a FREE book you can't get anywhere else: www.authoremmabray.com.

Keep reading for an excerpt of Taken by the Felon by Emma Bray.

Chapter 1

Ajax

My chest tightens painfully as I watch the live camera feed of my little angel sleeping sweetly in her bed. Her bed is a soft pink with lacy ruffles, and there's a gauzy white canopy hanging down all around it. She sleeps in a beautiful princess bed, looking exactly like a piece of candy at the store that your mother told you you couldn't have, yet you still wanted to reach out and slip it into your pocket when no one was looking, the temptation that you longed to take for yourself even if you knew you couldn't have it.

She's forbidden fruit.

If she was any younger, she'd be jailbait.

Of course, my Olivia isn't jailbait. She's legal—barely legal but legal. I made sure to ask her the first time I laid eyes on her and my cock got harder than a steel rod in my pants.

I've never felt such a potent surge of lust crash through me at the mere sight of a woman. The first time she skipped over to me with that long, honey-colored hair, those innocent blue eyes, and that tight young body that's enough to get me locked back up, precum started leaking out of my cock. That's something that's never happened to me before. Just looking at a woman has never been enough to have me ready to bust all in my pants like an untried schoolboy, but Olivia…

Fuck, Olivia…

She's the prettiest, most perfect little thing I've ever seen.

She'd be worth going to jail for…

Those kinds of thoughts should scare me. I never want to be locked up again. Being in the pen is a bitch.

I roll my shoulders and stretch my arms out in front of me, cracking my knuckles.

I was always buff, but I'm even more muscular now after my stint in the pen. I've always lifted weights, but in prison, there's nothing to do to make the time pass other than work out, which I did incessantly.

My body is a well-honed machine. I know I'm a big, scary-looking motherfucker, but Olivia—sweet, beautiful Olivia—has never been afraid of me. No, she skipped right up to that fence that separates her house from the lawn I mow and introduced herself and proceeded to chatter away like she didn't have a care in the world—like she couldn't see all the prison tattoos decorating my bare chest and both arms.

She's the first person since I've gotten out who's treated me like a normal human being, who didn't give me wary eyes for being so big and bulky, who didn't immediately look at me like what I am—a felon.

It wasn't hard to slip past her parents' security system and bug the house while they were away. Oh, I have no interest in watching what her parents are doing, but I need to be able to see Olivia at all times so I can make sure she's okay. I of all people know the terrors that can happen to a young girl, even if she thinks she's safe in her own home.

My jaw clenches as I think back on the reason I went to prison in the first place. That's never going to happen to my Olivia. Not on my watch. I might not have been able to protect my sister, but I got vengeance for her.

I know Olivia's parents warned her away from me. I can still remember her father's mask of rage and the suspicious look on his face when he came outside and saw his innocent young daughter talking to me across the fence that separated his yard from his neighbor's.

I knew right then and there that I'd never be cutting

his lawn or doing any sort of work for him. The man doesn't want me anywhere near his daughter, and I can't say I really blame the guy based on my criminal record alone. It's only one conviction, but it's a pretty big one. Olivia's father is another one of those who judge without knowing the full story.

Not Olivia, though. She didn't heed her father's warning. No, my pretty little princess kept sneaking out to come talk to me while I worked. It doesn't matter if it's sunny outside or not because her smile is enough to light up my entire world on the gloomiest day. I live for those moments when she comes skipping out the back door and prances over to the fence with that beautiful smile.

God, the first time she said my name in that pretty little voice, I swear I came *this* close to nutting in my pants. I definitely shot a stream of precum. I went home with a stain on my boxers and then jacked off three times in a row to the memory of her voice saying my name.

And that's what she does to me. I don't even have to imagine her naked. I can just picture her little face, remember the way her breathy little voice sounds, and that's enough to have me coming harder than I've ever come in my entire life.

I know she wants me too. I see the way her eyes flick over my shoulders and my bare chest. I see the way she bites her lip when sweat glistens on my skin. I even see the way she smashes those pretty little thighs together like she's trying to ease the ache between them. I'd bet my life the poor baby has never had a proper orgasm before. She might not even know what her body needs, but I sure as hell do, and I'd give my life to give it to her.

My cock is always so hard every time I'm around her. All she has to do is be in my presence, and the fucker is trying to bust through my pants, straining to get to what I already know is an unpopped little cherry, and dammit, that is *my* cherry. It's *mine* to pop.

The thought of another man stuffing his dick between her thighs makes me murderous with rage. I know Olivia feels this pull between us. That's why she disobeyed her father and sneaks out to come speak a few words to me when she sees me working at the house next door.

Olivia is a good girl. She just graduated high school, and she was always a straight-A student. Her parents have it planned for her to go to college, but something tells me that's not what she wants to do. She looks less than enthusiastic when she talks about her future at the university.

Yes, I know she wants me too, but a lifetime of falling in line and doing what her parents have told her to do is holding her back. She might sneak out for a few moments to speak to me across the fence, but she's not brave enough to jump across that line yet. Every time I've asked her to sneak away with me, let me take her out for a bite to eat or a walk in the park or *anything*—anything just to get her alone and spend some time with her without having to look over our shoulders for her parents—she bites her lip, her eyes looking torn and sadly declines, saying that she's sorry but she can't. I can see in her eyes that she truly is.

That's why I don't give her a hard time about it. I've contented myself with watching her from afar and taking whatever crumbs she throws me. I'm like a dog desperate for anything I can get from her. I'll be in her life however I can take it. I'm her silent protector, watching her over the live feeds I have set up in her house, and when she goes out, I'm in the shadows, following an unseen distance behind her to make sure nobody messes with my girl.

And I truly was content with that—until tonight. Until I saw her slip her fingers underneath her little cotton panties. I watched her stroke that little virgin pussy. I could tell she was unsure of what to do, just following her instincts, and god help me, but I couldn't stop myself from pulling my hard cock from my pants and stroking along with her.

I was ready to nut after three pumps, but I held back, only wanting to come when she did, and when she came and whispered my name on her lips, my spend ripped up violently from my balls and shot three feet in the air with my surprise.

Knowing that she was thinking of *me* when she was touching herself, that thoughts of *me* are what ultimately got her off, that's what ultimately sealed my decision. It was a game-changer.

Olivia isn't brave enough to be with me on her own. She's too afraid of disobeying her parents and disappointing them to make that decision on her own.

So, I'll make it for her.

Want more Emma Bray? Go to www.authoremmabray.com.